SUPER LISU
THE LOCUST ATTACK

YOLANDA CHAKAVA

Illustrated by
The Tsunami Studio

Published by

East African Educational Publishers Ltd.

Shreeji Road, off North Airport Road,

Embakasi, Nairobi.

P.O. Box 45314 – 00100, Nairobi, KENYA

Tel: +254 20 2324760

Mobile: +254 722 205661 / 722 207216 / 734 652012

WhatsApp: +254 722 205660

Email: eaep@eastafricanpublishers.com

Website: www.eastafricanpublishers.com

First published 2022

ISBN 978-9966-56-771-0

BOOKS IN THE SUPER LISU SERIES

1. **Super Lisu:** My Super Hair

2. **Super Lisu:** Colouring Book

3. **Super Lisu:** The Locust Attack

DEDICATION

To my sisters, Sharon and Andia –
my anchors and loudest cheerleaders.
Thank you.

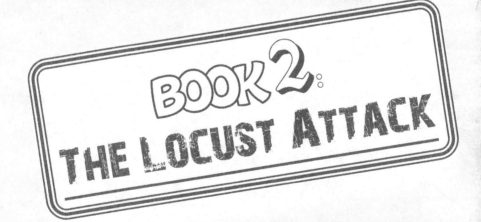

BOOK 2:
THE LOCUST ATTACK

CHAPTER ONE

"Run Kendi, RUN!" the crowd shouted.

So, I ran.

It was our school sports day.
I was leading the 100 metres final race.

I looked back over my shoulder. I was SO far ahead!

A flashback reminded me of the day I discovered my super hair, or 'D-Day' as I like to call it. Before D-DAY, I was an ordinary girl living an ordinary life. I had NEVER won anything!

D-DAY was exactly one year ago today.

It still felt unreal.

I crossed the finish line, waving my arms in the air. The crowd erupted in cheers and songs. The mood was electric.

My teammates surrounded me. They sang and danced to my favourite song, edited with my name:

Mama Kendi (Kendi)
Kendi Bonyo (Bonyo)
Bonyo simsim (simsim)
Yellow House wapi (wapi)?
Yellow House juu (juu)!

Melo, the team captain, patted me on the back. The COOL KIDS high-fived me. All the attention was on ME!

For the first time in my life, I was POPULAR. My head was buzzing.

I sang and danced. I was overjoyed!

From the corner of my eye, I noticed Chogo running towards me.

Chogo is my best friend and my neighbour.
He is eleven.

hongera – congratulations

Suddenly, I panicked. I am POPULAR now. What would the COOL KIDS think if they knew I was friends with Chogo?

I made a quick decision. I turned my head and snubbed him.

I did not see the sad look on Chogo's face.

I thought being popular
was EVERYTHING.
I would soon realise, that
was my FIRST mistake.

CHAPTER TWO

Sports day ended. Yellow House was declared the winner.

My throat ached from all the singing, but I did not care. I was on a winning high.

The party was in full swing.

Just then, a voice called me from the sidelines.

"Home time, Kendi!"

As I walked towards the voice, I had a nagging feeling that I had forgotten ...

I searched the crowd and spotted him in the distance.
When I was sure nobody was looking, I waved.

His expression remained blank.

I waved again, more forcefully this time. I was sure I had his attention now.

Nothing. Still blank.

Chogo looked me straight in the eye. Then he turned away.

I stared in shock.

waaaa – a Sheng' word to show shock or surprise

Before I could process what had just happened, the voice distracted me.

"Well done, Kendi!"

My eyes shifted to baba, standing in front of me.

"Thank you," I mumbled. I absentmindedly handed him my gold trophy for inspection.

"Where is Chogo? I thought he was coming home with us," baba said.

I searched the crowd again.

Chogo was gone.

baba - father

"No idea," I shrugged, "he must have found another ride home."

Anger was building up inside me.

"Chogo did not tell you he was leaving?" baba asked, confused.

"Nope," I said, avoiding eye contact.

"That is unlike Chogo," he murmured.

I hesitated. "Well ... he might be jealous because I am POPULAR now," I blurted out.

"Chogo? Jealous? WHY would you think that?" baba asked with an amused smile, fuelling my anger.

"Never mind," I snapped.

"Kendi, Chogo is your best friend," he said slowly, "unless ... YOU ... did something ...?"

A heavy silence filled the air. I held out until it became unbearable. "Well, maybe I do not NEED a best friend," I muttered.

He gave me a stern look. "You are mistaken, Kendi," baba warned.

I crossed my arms in defiance.

"Can we go home now?" I asked, changing the subject. I did not want to talk about Chogo.

"OK," he replied coldly.

I did not see the disappointed look on his face.

Images of the race, the cheers and the dancing occupied my mind. I smiled to myself, lost in thought.

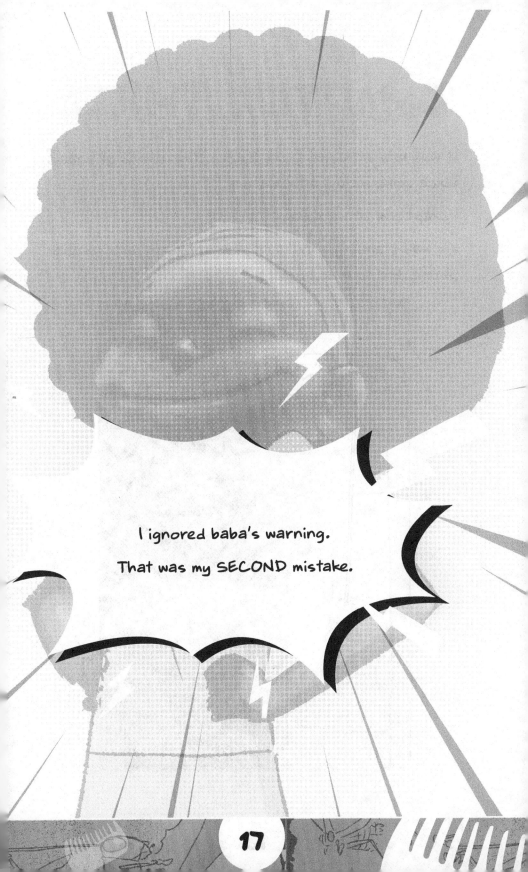

CHAPTER THREE

It was late at night. I was asleep. The sound of baba's voice woke me up with a start.

I crept out of my room.

He was standing in the living room, talking on his mobile phone. He sounded upset.

A voice on the other side of the line responded.

"Oh dear. This is a DISASTER!" baba cried. He slumped into the sofa.

I stepped forward to hear more. I did not look where I was going.

I landed hard on the floor.

"Kendi, what are you doing?" baba asked, startled.

"Sorry ... I tripped," I stammered.

"I will call you back," he whispered quickly into the phone and disconnected the call.

"Did I wake you up?" he asked.

"Umm ... kind of ... but it is fine," I replied quickly.
"What is wrong?" I asked.

"Nothing," he said hesitantly. "It will be fine in the morning."

His unsure tone raised my suspicion.

"Go to sleep now, Kendi," he said more firmly. "It is late."

I reluctantly returned to my room. As I drifted back to sleep, I wondered what news could have made baba so anxious.

When my eyes opened again, it was bright outside.

I dragged myself out of bed. I could hear the TV on full blast.

I found him standing in the living room, eyes glued to the TV.

I knew then, something was very wrong.

CHAPTER FOUR

"Baba?" I called cautiously.

Slowly, he turned to face me. He looked shocked and terrified at the same time.

He pointed at the TV.

"WHO is coming?" I asked.

I looked at the TV. My mouth opened but no words came out.

We watched in silence.

Finally, the words came.

"LOCUSTS!" baba shouted back. "THEY are locusts," he said, catching his breath.

I rubbed my eyes, not believing what I was seeing.

He nodded, eyes still glued to the TV.

"But ... locusts do not look like THAT!" I exclaimed.

"WHY are they SO BIG ... and SO MANY!" I cried.

"It is a swarm of desert locusts," he replied. "We have never seen them before in Kenya. It is all the heavy rain at the wrong time of the year." He shrugged. "As the climate is changing, strange things are happening."

"Is this what you were talking about last night?" I asked.

"Yes," he sighed. "I was talking to your Grandma. They invaded our farm in Kitui County and ate ALL the maize. There is nothing left."

"Is Grandma safe?" I asked.

"Yes," he nodded. "But she is afraid. She said ... she said ..." he paused, trying to find the right words. "She said ... they keep growing BIGGER, but I told her that is IMPOSSIBLE!"

We both turned to the TV. A news presenter was now interviewing one of the farmers.

"These locusts are NOT normal!" the farmer exclaimed. "They are TOO BIG and ... STILL GROWING!"

The news presenter pointed at the sky. "LOOK!"

I squinted at the TV.

Right before our eyes, the locusts were SERIOUSLY growing.

"How is this possible?" I wondered aloud.

Suddenly, the camera flipped back to the presenter.

"The locusts have eaten EVERYTHING in Kitui County and are MOVING FAST!" she yelled. "Food is running out! The President has declared a national emergency!"

Baba gasped.

The news headline was big and bold at the centre of the screen.

CHAPTER FIVE

My heart was pounding.

I exchanged a knowing look with baba. He did not move.

I raced to the door.

I stopped and faced him.

"I need to go, baba," I said. "I need to stop the locusts before they destroy EVERYTHING. If I do not, soon we will all starve."

I did not recognise my own voice. I sounded so ... so ... sure of myself. I tried to hide my own surprise.

Baba cleared his throat. "Kendi, are you REALLY sure about this?"

"Yes, baba." I nodded.

I was SURE. This was the moment I had been waiting for. MY FIRST MISSION.

He remained quiet. He knew I was right.

"Well," he said finally. "You cannot go out like THAT."

I forgot I was still wearing my pyjamas.

"I ... I do not have anything else to wear," I said, flustered.

"Yes, you do," he smiled. "I will be right back."

I glanced at the TV impatiently. The locusts had reached Machakos County.

"Here you go!" I heard baba's voice behind me. He sounded excited.

I spun around and looked at what he was carrying.

"This is your SUPER LISU costume. I was waiting for the right time to give it to you," he said. "I guess that time is now ..." His voice trailed off.

My eyes widened with excitement. I hurriedly fitted it on.

"I made it out of your mama's favourite material and beads," he said proudly. "She would be so proud of you right now," he added, smiling fondly.

I stared at my reflection in the mirror. I had so many questions about mama ...

"This is starting to feel very REAL," I said quietly. I had practised using my powers, secretly wondering if I would ever need to use them again.

Baba gave me an encouraging nudge.

Could this be a dream? I pinched myself to be sure.

I winced. DEFINITELY REAL.

Shouting and commotion interrupted us.

I snapped back to attention. Images of Nairobi residents raiding supermarkets filled the TV screen. Baba and I looked at each other.

"Are you ready for your first mission?" he asked anxiously.

At the time, I REALLY thought I was ready.

CHAPTER SiX

"So, what is your plan?" baba asked.

"Umm ..." I hesitated. "Plan?"

"You have a plan, right?" He raised his eyebrows.

I did not have a plan.

"I will wing it," I said, waving my hand dismissively.

"Kendi, you NEED a plan!" he cried in frustration.

I knew that tone.

"Relax, baba!" I cut him off. "I am about to take down some locusts!"

I was out of the door before he could respond.

I smiled confidently to myself. What could go wrong?

I underestimated the danger.
That was my THIRD mistake.

CHAPTER SEVEN

I summoned one of my five powers. "Flybraids, take me to the border of Nairobi County and Machakos County," I said. I shook my head.

A shimmer passed through my hair. As my hairstyle changed, it glowed ...

Up, up and away I went!

I spotted the General Service Unit (GSU) barricade. The officers were frantic. The air was full of tear gas.

I looked far ahead. I could see a big dark cloud approaching. The LOCUSTS!

The tear gas was not working.

I needed to act NOW!

I crossed the barricade and positioned myself in front of the GSU officers.

At first, nobody noticed me.

Then one officer bumped me from behind, as more charged forward.

"We msichana toka hapa!" she said angrily.

I frowned. Did she REALLY think I was here to play?

We msichana toka hapa – get out of here, young girl

Hii si saa ya mchezo – now is not time for games

Time to use a second power. "Cornrow energy, create a barricade to trap the locusts at Nairobi County border with Machakos County. Stop the attack," I murmured. I shook my head.

A shimmer ... my hairstyle changed ... it glowed ...

Energy beams lifted from my hair and created a barricade.

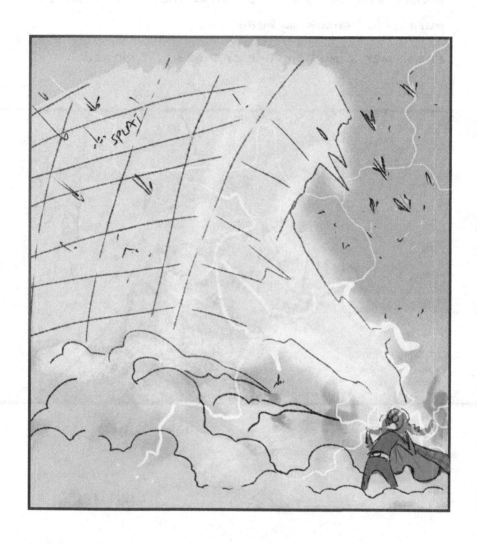

There was stunned silence.

The GSU officers stopped and stared at the energy beams.

Eyes darted everywhere, searching for the source.

More and more curious stares were landing on me.

I smiled proudly. The little voices in my head were screaming.

I waited for singing and dancing to follow.

Nothing.

A strange, eerie silence filled the air.

Something was different ... something was NOT right.

My smile faded. I looked around anxiously.

And then ... I heard it.

CHAPTER EIGHT

"LOOOOOOK!" a voice screamed.
I tried to look but I felt too dizzy ... WEAK.
My legs buckled.

The commotion started again. Running ... voices ...
tear gas, which looked even thicker now.

"Msichana ... I told you NOT to play here!" Her again.
The same GSU officer shouted in my ear.

msichana - young girl

I stumbled ... confused ... dazed. My eyes stung. Slowly, I looked up ...
My energy beams were fading. The air was thick, heavy with tear gas.

With each POP, more locusts broke through my barricade.
I did not stop the locusts. I only slowed them down.

The locusts were strong ... MUCH stronger than I had anticipated.

I stared at the scene in confusion.

The locusts were destroying EVERYTHING!

The GSU officers were now yelling at me from all directions.

toka hapa – get out of here

I closed my eyes and held back the tears that were threatening to fall.
WHY did I not win? WHY did I not stop the locusts? I wondered.

Unexpectedly, the answer hit me in the face. My three mistakes unfolded right before my eyes.

1. Popularity is not everything.
2. I ignored Baba's warnings.
3. I had no plan.

I looked around helplessly. Baba's warning was playing on repeat in my head.

I did not want to be popular anymore. I needed a friend.

I searched the crowd, unsure of who I was looking for.

I realised I was alone.

My barricade would not hold. Reality dawned on me.

EVERYTHING would be destroyed.

My first mission was going to fail.

CHAPTER NINE

I burst into the apartment. Baba was pacing the living room frantically.

I ran into his arms. My tears started flowing freely.

"I messed up baba!" I sobbed. "I have failed in my first mission!"

"Tell me what happened, Kendi," he said softly.

I told him everything.

"I was SO excited about being popular. I wanted to be one of the cool kids. Now I know that none of that is important. I wish I had listened to you ..." I rambled on.

He listened quietly. I had no idea if he understood any of what I was saying.

"I do not want to be popular anymore!" I cried out eventually.

I felt a great sense of relief once all the words came out. I wiped my tears, took a deep breath and waited.

Baba studied me carefully before he spoke. "Kendi, you have learnt important lessons. Yes, being POPULAR can be cool, but it comes at a high price. Super Lisu is NOT about being one of the COOL KIDS. It is about doing the right thing."

"I know that now. I am sorry I did not listen. I failed."
My shoulders slumped.

He smiled. "Kendi, you have a lot to learn, AND, you
will. Do not give up on yourself, OK?"

"Thanks, baba." I gave him a big hug.

"Now, I think there is someone else you owe an
apology," he said.

I nodded. "I will be right back."

CHAPTER TEN

I knocked loudly on the door.

No answer.

Just as I raised my hand to knock again, the door opened.

Chogo stood before me with a stern face.

I spoke quickly.

"Chogo, I thought being popular was SO COOL. I was wrong. I am sorry for the way I acted. You are my best friend."

I waited for his response.

Nothing. His face was expressionless.

I was panic-stricken.

I was about to give up. Then, he spoke.

"You hurt my feelings, Kendi," he said softly.

"I know." I looked down, ashamed.

"Lately ... you ... you have changed," he said carefully.

I froze. "What do you mean?" I asked. I knew exactly what he meant.

He shrugged. "I cannot put my finger on it, but you are definitely ... different." He looked me straight in the eye.

Caught off guard, I was tempted to tell Chogo EVERYTHING.

"I ... I ... am ... um ... I ... am ... asking you to PLEASE forgive me," I said, biting my tongue at the last second.

No response.

"Thank you, Kendi. I forgive you," he said finally. "You are my best friend too."

I reached up and gave him a hug.

For a moment, I forgot about the chaos outside.

CHAPTER ELEVEN

"Kendi! Have you seen the news?" Chogo asked.

He pulled me inside the apartment before I could respond.

Something in Chogo's voice grabbed my interest.

He opened his laptop. Chogo was a whizz at computers.

"The locusts. They are growing," he said as he typed on the laptop.

I smirked. "EVERYONE knows that."

He ignored me and kept typing. I continued watching him curiously.

"Not EVERYONE knows WHY," he continued. "I have been watching the locust videos people are uploading online." He turned the screen towards me. "It is NOT adding up."

"What do you mean?" I asked. He had my full attention now.

He played one video in slow motion. "Look closely," he said. We watched the locusts get bigger and bigger.

"I think SOMETHING is making them grow ..."

"Chogo!" I cut him off sharply.

Chogo froze the screen obediently.

"Play it back!" I commanded.

We watched the replay in silence.

My heartbeat quickened as the image became clearer.
What I saw gave me goosebumps.

"What?" Chogo asked, confused.

No, I could not tell Chogo my suspicions, not until I was sure.

"The TEAR GAS," I whispered.

Chogo looked at me, even more confused.

"Look what happens when the locusts meet the tear gas," I said impatiently.

Ati - a Swahili word that shows surprise. It is also used to clarify information.

Chogo watched.

"They get BIGGER!" he exclaimed in disbelief. "How did you see that?"

I barely heard him. My eyes were glued to the corner of the screen.

An almost invisible mystery person, dressed in a dark hoodie, lurked behind a cloud of gas. I knew it at once.

I squinted at the screen for one last confirmation.

Yes ... SHE was laughing.

"What is the fastest way to clear tear gas from the air?" I asked quickly. My mind was racing.

Chogo turned back to his laptop and continued typing. "Well, it says here you need fresh air. I guess you would need A LOT of air, wind and energy ..." His voice trailed off.

"Wind ... energy ..." I jumped from the chair in excitement.

"Got WHAT?" Chogo shook his head sadly. "That is impossible, Kendi ... we are doomed."
I ran out of the door, leaving a stunned Chogo. I made a mental note to thank him later.

This was the breakthrough I needed. I had one more chance to stop the locust attack.

CHAPTER TWELVE

Baba's face lit up when he saw me, sensing a shift in my energy.

I quickly filled him in on Chogo's video, leaving out the ONE important detail I was not ready to share yet. No, NOT YET.

Baba glanced at the TV. I knew what he was thinking.

"So, what happens now?" he asked.

I smiled broadly. "I have a plan."

I was back at the Nairobi-Machakos border in no time. Things were worse, MUCH worse than I left them. The border was engulfed in gas.

The locusts were HUGE! I cringed at the sight. I am NOT a fan of insects.

I focused on my plan. Just as I was about to shake my head, I heard a VERY WICKED laugh behind me.

I shivered. My body sensed the danger immediately.

I turned around slowly.

There she stood. Her face was partially hidden but there was no mistaking her. SHE was the mystery person from the video.

She pointed in my direction.
I gritted my teeth. "WHO ARE YOU?" I shouted. She did not look much bigger than me.
Silence.
Our eyes locked.

Then she raised her hands ... to strike.

Instinctively, I ducked. I was fast, but not fast enough.

A ball of tear gas engulfed me. My eyes stung. I coughed, gasping for air.

Blinded by the tear gas, my hands swung wildly, groping for something ... anything ...

I heard her laugh EVEN LOUDER at my distress.

In a rage, I charged into the darkness.

I emerged from a cloud of gas, ready to strike back.

To my surprise, nobody was there.

I scanned the crowd, knowing it was pointless. SHE was gone.

I had a nagging feeling something about her was familiar. I had no idea why.

I brushed my thoughts aside. I needed to focus on my plan before it was too late to stop the attack.

CHAPTER THIRTEEN

I knew exactly where to get huge amounts of wind energy.

"This plan better work," I whispered to myself. "Here goes nothing."

"Cornrow energy, power the 365 wind turbines at Lake Turkana Wind Power Station to clean the air," I said and shook my head, HARD.

A shimmer ... my hairstyle changed ... it glowed ...

I waited ...

Then ... I heard it.

The energy blasts from the largest wind farm in Africa were powerful. Strong winds of fresh air from Lake Turkana Wind Power Station gushed towards the scene.

This time, my powers held strong. The wind gained momentum.

Cars, matatus and buses stopped on the side of the road. The wind was too strong for them to drive.
The wind reached the barricade. GSU officers downed their tools and ran for cover.
The locusts were disappearing.

I stood firm.
After what felt like FOREVER, suddenly there was silence.

matatu - minibus

The tear gas cleared. The swarm of locusts disappeared.

I ALMOST could not believe it.

A familiar, clear blue sky emerged.

I smiled proudly.

I left the scene quickly before GSU officers emerged. I was no longer interested in attracting attention. I had learnt my lesson.

At that moment, I realised I was exhausted, but it was TOTALLY worth it.

I headed home with a smile on my face.

Everyone was now safe.

CHAPTER FOURTEEN

Baba and I lay spread out on the sofa, watching the 7:00 pm news.

Reports were coming in from everywhere. Blasts of fresh air were being used to target locusts across the country. The President declared wind energy projects a 'national priority' to stop the spread of locusts.

The media was full of questions.

We listened and laughed at each new twist.

"So," baba said, breaking the silence. "How did you do it?"

I smiled. "I have been reading about Lake Turkana, the source of my powers. Then I came across a story about Lake Turkana Wind Power Station. It sounded SO COOL! When Chogo said we needed clean energy to get rid of the desert locusts, I do not know how, but I just knew what I needed to do."

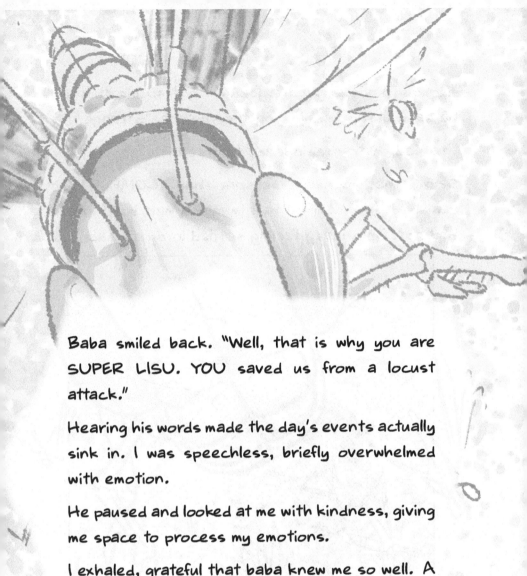

Baba smiled back. "Well, that is why you are SUPER LISU. YOU saved us from a locust attack."

Hearing his words made the day's events actually sink in. I was speechless, briefly overwhelmed with emotion.

He paused and looked at me with kindness, giving me space to process my emotions.

I exhaled, grateful that baba knew me so well. A comfortable silence passed between us.

"Nobody knows why the locusts got so big though," he said, abruptly changing the subject. "Strange."

I tensed. "Strange, indeed," I agreed.

SHE, the mystery person, had COMPLETELY vanished. Almost like I had imagined her, but I knew I had not. An uneasy feeling settled in my stomach.

"I am proud of you, Kendi," baba said softly, interrupting my thoughts. "I am sure your mama is proud of you too."

The question I had been dying to ask for so long finally spilled out.

WHAT HAPPENED TO MAMA?

He shifted uncomfortably on the sofa.

"I ... I do not know," he said finally.

"PLEASE ... tell ... me ... what happened," I said, trying my best not to sound desperate. I failed.

He nodded, hearing the strain in my voice.

I braced myself. Something told me my story was about to get more ... complicated.

Printed in the United States
by Baker & Taylor Publisher Services